YOUNG HEARTS

RUN FREE

RANCE REDMAN

MANUFACTURED IN THE UNITED STATES OF AMERICA

PUBLISHED BY SOUTHERN PLEASURES BOOKS

Distribution in the United Kingdom By
Lightning Source UK Ltd.
6 Precedent Drive
Rooksley
Milton Keynes
MK13 8PR, UK
UNITED KINGDOM

LIBRARY OF CONGRESS DATA

REDMAN, RANCE C.
YOUNG HEARTS RUN FREE / BY C. RANCE
REDMAN. - 1ST ed.

Library of Congress Control Number:
2008900893
FIRST EDITION: FEBRUARY 2008
ISBN 978-0-6151-9041-9
(PAPERBACK)
(CLOTH)

COVER BY SOUTHERN PLEASURES BOOKS

This book is dedicated to young Hearts with teachers who never came to class, yet nevertheless taught every subject well.

Thanks Albert Murray

Thanks Brown Eyes

Thanks Renee

Thanks Felix

young hearts run free

CHAPTER I

Campus Visit

RANCE REDMAN

FORGIVENESS IS OUR FREEDOM

Campus Visit

I KILLED MY FATHER.

Dimly lit by the slowly descending orange sun, the road cluttered with chunks of mud rocks hitting the base of the trotting bus seemed to stretch about the dell endlessly. As the hot eye of God wilted a pungent scent from magnolia trees, the deeply crimson colored trail looked minute in comparison to the towering weeping willows gracefully bowing with spots of Spanish moss peeking through their leaves.

Peering through the dust haze covered window like a child with an oversized spyglass in hand, my consciousness digressed to another world as cracking pecans sounded as they were pushed to the ground by light temperate gusts of wind. All that was etched in my view at that instant were all of the things that codified *South* in my lasting memory.

For it was here I became a man. It was here I fell in *love*. It was here I found my enduring passion for my musical virtuosity. Frustrated with rejection of my permanent cloak of dark hue, it was here I was introduced to *rebels* without a just cause. It was here I began to chart a course of legacy renewed for my surname.

But at that moment, my only object of interest was the peaceful consolation of cirrus clouds in an undulating marble-like sky, which helped me to escape two silent catalysts for death- the excessive weights of *rage* and *sorrow*. Not withstanding the brief reminiscence of nostalgia, encamped within the confines of the small iron coach I was on my way to view mortality in my likeness- the grave of my father.

The affinity of a man I barely knew, I, his spitting image would have to stand over it to come to grips; I would have to accept that there would never be reconciliation. Time was our foe and it won.

Despite whatever hesitant adversity I felt in my heart, I exceeded my reservations hoping to face my demon (the lurking, ever nudging fact that I hated an invisible man, and the possibility that he too hated me).

The South cradled my evolution and helped me to avoid its nuisance- a fact cultivating an incomplete *heart* perforated with chances untaken. Formidably, I expected this day to come, but the notion that I would not be affected gave me a boundless impermeable arrogance keeping me less concerned with him succumbing to his fate. You see, I killed him, and I was *free*.

CHAPTER II

ENROLLMENT

RANCE REDMAN

AVOIDANCE CONTRACTS OUR BEAT

Enrollment

I ARRIVED IN A desperate *run* from Detroit: a decaying debacle made of promise unseen. My plane landed to thankful prayers early in the morning after a short transfer in Memphis. Dressed to impress in a fully formal designer suit, bearing only sixty dollars in my pocket, I foolishly reached hot Alabama the second week of August.

Heat emitted from the Montgomery Airport landing strip pavement, bringing a blurring sight of the beating horizon. My white dress shirt soon soaked in perspiration in the time I waited for the conveyor belt to swing around my luggage. Making my way down the sparsely decorated corridor's unpadded industrial carpet, I met my contact arranged by my high school counselor to escort me to the university. We made little conversation during the ride, and before long the royal blue mustang convertible he drove ascended the shade-covered street called *Jackson*.

Nested between cultural barren and null distortion of history somewhere laid an oasis of nurturing enlightenment. Centered in verdures of grassy green panoramas, ocher bricks, and quadrangles sat an artist's representation of the earth's equinox- the time of year when all parts of the day and night are of equal length in all parts of the earth.

Here our common frame was knowledge. Here the clash of the urbanized children of the "Great Migration" generation and Southern rural blacks is united to take on the arduous journey of HBCU.

Here, realistically unfettered feet of slave descendants mock true pursuit of enlightenment in exchange for the bling of financial aid checks, and forced goals of parental birthright place their offspring into the modern middle class status quo. Here the young mindset *abandons* true cultural exploration in search for the capitalist lifestyle outside of their void poor neighborhoods. There were few who sought to return to uplift struggling dreamless *hearts* that on a daily basis are jailed in their ghettos and barrios of miseducation and lack luster prisons of the mind. Here young *hearts* ran free.

Perched atop a hill was its emblem, a hall ironically named in honor of its donor- a Ku Klux Klan imperial wizard who sought to give money during his run for governor. The school was blotted with beautiful flowers of unfamiliar yellows and purples and rust red soil filming the bases of gargantuan academic structures.

Everything was overwhelmingly new- the way the Southerners spoke, the way they walked, their gentle smiles, and their stern looks of consternation for northern ire.

Black faces of myriad colors walked the "yard" with nappy rooted afros that were twisted, corn rolled, braided, and cut low. Long t-shirts covered baggy pants sagging over white shoes, and oversized sports caps covered tied durags. Traditional prep khakis and golf shirts intermingled with tight blue jeans and sundresses.

To the deafening bass and faint lyrics of hip-hop tunes blasting from cruising automobiles, I made my way to Card Hall- a dank historic edifice of poor dated architecture prescribed to incoming freshman males.

"Nice suit there", I heard launching from a small office slide glass window.

"How many buttons are on the arm of the coat?" bombarded by an aged voice I later grew to know as Mr. Greathouse. His drooping jowls speckled with sunspots slumped with the unthreatening invitation of a grandfather. Thin glasses resting upon high cheekbones circled the leathered face of the dorm director as he rose to greet me.

Countenance for authority always posed problematic for me. Typically I felt relegated in its presence, and often I rebelled at the onset of anxiety. Usually I found myself throwing in the towel on relations requiring respect for older male figures, and I distrusted every man I ever knew.

(Mr. Greathouse was bop. His offbeat phrases ended on weak beats of questions between definitive strong answers. He was one of many who were genuinely concerned about the matriculation of students at HBCU. His words of encouragement may have been unintentional, but very often soothed the souls of young hearts in a foreign land. Shedding naivety is never easy, and his subtle acts of support gave credence to the concept of responsible higher education for African Americans. I respected him.)

"Three", I replied in a timid, yet questioning return, fearful of speaking to any staff of authority.

Good…

Three or more…

That's how you know that you have a nice suit…

I wish my son made an impression like that when steps in a room…

I can tell that you will *do great things* here...

Welcome to HBCU... he stated in idle small talk while checking me onto the roster.

Intimidated by the prowess of upperclassmen and brawny athletes seeming larger than life with big protruding chests and voices with timbres of African chiefs, I pressed through the lobby. Passing reupholstered chairs, a stained microwave, and vending machines I dragged my bags behind me. Looking on a note taped to a huge metal key baring my room number, I was led to the third floor.

I pushed the scratched brown painted wooden door to view of a water-puddled cubical in which I was to spend the next nine months. A cold blue plastic covered mattress sat elevated on an iron bed frame low to the floor, and above it, a desk teetered on bent metal legs topped with etched graffiti. Anticipating the only fearful disappointment I could face, I awaited a roommate resembling the quality of my housing accommodations.

Eager to peel out the clammy suit, I unpacked some personal items and headed for the shower. I slipped on my rubber flip-flops and cotton towel, and squeaked to the community bathroom on the opposite side of the hallway.

The large room was equipped with four spout heads, partitioned toilets, and an equal number of toothpaste-covered sinks. *(I recall the steam that would seep under the door seal fogging the kick panel, causing water to accumulate on our room floor. The cesspools in unclean commodes would sicken us to our stomachs when the air conditioning failed, and the clogged drain holes in the shower would overflow onto our feet when we bathed.)*

I quickly half dried off and hastened to my door hoping to avoid any potential voyeurs. Standing in my room brown body naked with beaded water streaming down my stomach, I realized I had not unpacked my clothing when I heard the lock snap behind me.

CHAPTER III

UNPACKING

IGNORANCE IS OUR ATTACKER

Unpacking

I QUICKLY TURNED, FACING an older woman
standing in door arch holding a cardboard box that she dropped to
the floor. "I'm sorry! My son is on his way up the stairs!" she
yelled hurriedly closing the door. Less embarrassed as she, I
slipped on some running shorts and turned the knob. Shirtless
with extended hand, I introduced myself.

"Heart, from Detroit", I said smiling. She drew back the
corners of her mouth, head bowed, eyes facing upward.

"Mrs. Davis", daintily shaking the tips of my fingers.

"Rod is on his way up. He's a sophomore from Chicago."

That moment, standing in the foreground of the freshly
pale painted hall, next to an inoperable patina water fountain

oxidized bright teal, was Rod Davis- a lanky, bony, coffee figure appearing in an extra long black shirt with a white italicized "*R*" in its center. A sinister grin exposed a devious side contrary to his softer baby face and giant stature.

We exchanged "whuddups" and immediately deemed each other "D-town" and "Chi-town". He told me about the basketball student-athlete program, and of his major-athletic training. Relieved at his hometown demeanor, I explained my majoring in classical music performance.

We gradually broke the ice that day by consuming countless greasy pizza slices, Playstation matches, and an exhausting evening basketball game. We shot the breeze well into the night discussing pastimes: his love for basketball and my love of culture, his love for women and my love for travel. (*Chi-town was single-minded rap and I was eclectic jazz. Rap was following the commercialized paths that jazz now ran from. Separating itself from its basement party DJ's, rap is now just an unjustified means of social mutiny for suburban kids in order to glorify the prison epidemic and drug sales as the black man's only way of a bad life. Rap is the transmogrification of jazz form in a better life, but doesn't know it.*

Rap filled the vacuity of urban aesthetic when jazz suffered beyond its control corporate exploitation via the almighty dollar. Rap in due time will suffer the same fate if it

continues to align the obsession of capitalism with the perception
of beauty, eventually blindsiding cultural growth and masses of
souls that could be educated to our triumphant beautiful struggle
in America.

Rap neglects to contribute to the humanistic properties of
blueness in Blackness when it disassociates itself from its
previous forms- jazz, blues, gospel, R&B, country, rock, etc.
When we collate these forms of music we take notice that all of
the former experience in their singular tracks of evolution a
reoccurring demise. In watered down attempts to fit within the
folds of the mechanism of popular sales, we often alter these
forms and dismantle the basic structures that make American
music so greatly unique.

We stand today at the crux of vacillation. Do we no
longer victimize our art forms in service to larger social
atmospheres that exploit the shapeliness of black women and
overly aggressive male thugs with advertising craftiness? Do we
forge the front of electronic music rebellion and redefine the
parameters of our innovations? Do we stand stolidly idle? Young
hearts will decide.)

Rod wasn't from the *hood*, and therefore relished its
hardships. I was, and *ran* from its misery I knew all too well.
(Rap wasn't jazz's replacement; they were indeed the same- both

things running away trying to find themselves.) As quickly as we
identified with each other, we argued.

Please…

Sports and rap is just a reflection of our daily lives in the
Chi yo'…

I was irritated at his forced attempt to be *down.*

Yelling.

Right…how?

They're our only way out da' hood…

Proselytizing to end the argument.

If sports and rap are our only way out, then why are you
here? Plus…

You wear the clothes and the big medallion, but you are
afraid of people like me who live in the city past the
skyscrapers…

"Fuck you nigga, you think you're hard", he said in a
jovial manner.

"I'm from the Chi!" he laughed to hide his trepidation.

We both started laughing when the smell of mangos and
coconut breezed across the court. There standing to the sideline
was a young caramel colored female with hazel eyes.

"Damn" we pronounced simultaneously, gawking at her
voluptuous form.

"I like college already," I said in mid lay-up.

"You too?" he asked emphatically.

"That bitch is fine!" stroking his sweat dripping broad chin and squinting his eyes as if to gain a better look. Amazed at the passing of Southern baked backside, he sputtered, "I'll holla at you later Detroit", following her.

I gripped the ball with one hand and tucked it under my left arm and headed back to the room navigating through a lush courtyard with Spanish style black fortifying bars facing the rear of the dorm. I sat on my bed and leaned against the cold wall, drifting off from a long day. My eyes closed and reopened, focused on a neon digital clock on my desk that unexpectedly read 3:17AM. In the darkness I heard shifting, moaning, and hard breathing. Gathering my dizzy sight, I flicked the light switch.

Chi-town's 6'5 physique in tighty-whities extended off the end of the bed with his head between her slender thighs. One of her hands grasped his ears. One held a bra less breast. Clothes were tossed about; their tennis shoes were strewn cross the grimy floor. I froze.

Aroused being watched, as if it turned her on to see *my* erection, "Roommate are you down?" Rod motioned with his hand to join. "Like four flats on a Cadillac!" I replied. The girl from the courts stood looking up in nude elegance, pulling my Pistons jersey and wife beater tee to the side licking my nipple with her moist warm tongue.

My pulse raced. I suffocated as she grabbed my arm and Caesar hair cut frenching me. She backed to the light switch and soon, there we were- three beautiful summer tanned bodies with tongues and legs intertwined in sticky injections of touching, feeling, and tasting in the darkness.

Daylight arose. I never knew her name, but Chi-town and I jokingly called her "*a pick*" referring to the way that he picked her up at the court. It was the first of many initiations for *unknowns* starring D-town and Chi-town, which became rumored occurrences in the darkness on the third floor of Card Hall.

Soon we were cast into the roles of designated fantasy grantors at the behest of many *nameless picks* after games, after gigs, after parties, and after step shows who snuck pass Mr. Greathouse after visiting hours. We became popular legend because he was a towering athlete and I, the well endowed musician, swiftly budding into promiscuity and I had yet to unpack my belongings.

Unpacking proved difficult for me. In my youth, unable to afford the cost of childcare, my single mother was sometimes reduced to taking me along to work- places challenging her womanliness and color. *(My mother was third stream jazz. She often fell under scrutiny, as it was already difficult for her to maintain employment being prissy to blacks with her fair West Indian skin, and too black for whites. So when it was impossible*

to keep my improvisations in these places with her, I was left in
an empty house to explore and break things.)

When I burned myself in adolescent curiosity, I was sent
to stay with friends and relatives who advanced sex and were
physically abusive. "This year Latino friends on the *Southwest*
side sodomized me with objects…that year grandma's neighbor's
son in the *Hole* made me suck *it*…and this year a drunken uncle
on the *Eastside* slapped me…and that year the drug addict cousin
on the *Westside* did not feed me…" until I moved so often that
even as an adult in college, I still refused to unpack.

My clothing always rested in a bag or box for as long as I
could remember. Each time I comprised the gumption to be at
ease in folding my items in a dresser, I moved. So, I stopped
unpacking, believing placation to be a bad omen. My scholarship
paid for my dorm room annually, yet an anxiety forever smelted
in my heart kept me restless and uncomfortable even in my own
room, with my own bed, with my own closet, and my own
drawers to unpack my belongings. I feared unpacking like I
feared intimacy, authority, criticism, failure, and *manhood*.

YOUNG HEARTS RUN FREE

CHAPTER IV
REGISTRATION

YOUNG HEARTS RUN FREE

INDOLENCE IS OUR RENDERING

Registration

THE FIRST WEEKS OF classes came, and the sweltering degrees subsided into heavy autumnal rains; Rains that could literally be smelled and felt before the torrential bottom dropped from the sky happened often. In these days my nineteenth birthday passed without celebrated bravado. The weather was drab, yet I did not long for my precious *Renaissance City*.

Here I still had not attempted to call or write home as this place was my safe haven from the conflagrations of a hell I wished would vanish. Removing myself from Detroit, here I sheltered my hopes from a place cradling deviancy and connoted strife to be permanent. With the exception of my mother, I sheltered myself from a family frowning upon innovation, promoted antagonism to excellence, and had a value system leaving men to the powerless conformity of the convict, and women incapacitated in the rubble of the demised discarded domestic household.

(My family was avant-garde jazz. One had to approach them with a degree of open-mindedness. At first encounter they seemed ruthless and discombobulated, but the more attention paid, one noticed in their frustration they only searched for a new voice for freedom in the chaos of their composition. In their efforts they just became forms of formlessness because they abandoned educated foundations of tertian chords and distinct personal melodies of established historical concepts. Straying to a lost world of bewildering radicalism (drugs, violence, and poverty) they failed to find a new verse. My family's musicality of life was built on abstract imagination, and possessed little to no tradition, shirking it because it was vogue. The world's connoisseurs dismissed their potential as nonmusical because they did not fit within the functions of modern music. They lived and worked for moments of spontaneity, and cared less to understand the methodologies of their streams-of-conscience and formlessness. They in turn looked down upon the study of society's form because they themselves lacked the aptitude or chops to garner an established way.)

Running on zero energy, I was scheduled to take the English grammar exam required for all newcomers at the conclusion of orientation. Hoards of the casually dressed freshman class filed into the circular sports dome with a makeshift stage in the center to find a seat wherever they could. Flanked under black and gold past championship banners and extra-large stars and stripes, blank computer scan sheets, pencils, and booklets were shuffled down the aisles.

We nonchalantly filled in the bubbles and impatiently passed the booklets back to flee. The stout Vice President of Academic Affairs interrupted our exit and rose to the podium in her taupe dress to scattered applause and flagrant noise as she stumbled.

Excuse me. People… her words harshly echoed over microphone feedback and disruption.

You have been officially admitted to HBCU….

Congratulations!

Applause.

Do realize what a privilege you have by being here…

Running her fingers through her cliché professional hair, her pencil fell to the ground from her ear. The juvenile audience snickered and jeered.

Laugh if you will…she proclaimed,

But look to your friends at your side…

In a humorous glimpse to my left an impromptu sketcher was drawing a mustache on the VP's program photo; to my right a gentleman gingerly slept open-mouthed like a vagabond.

Realize that by graduation statistically two of you won't be here…

Fifty percent of you will one day see the walls of a jail cell…

America laughs at you when they say define *mass confusion*: Fathers Day in a Black neighborhood, she paused.

A hush fell as if a silence bomb dropped, and unexpectedly we were conscripted in every faction until her closing.

Using lists on the syllabi given by my professors, one day I proceeded to the long column of humans at the campus bookstore. Spending a great deal of time waiting to approach the doors, I was disappointed to learn I could not afford the price of books for the semester. Frustrated that I could not rely on parental intervention as my colleagues, I was reduced to retreating to the library to read the text on reserve before classes.

I was goggled as bazaar for intensely studying beyond the call of duty by my peers, yet I was eager to learn because I knew what I *stood to lose*. The purging of intellectualism by the manifold taking college for granted acerbated me, but did not dawdle my momentum. My professors doubted my pious impetus.

Leave my class now!

I asked you to bring your book…

I don't have the patience for shiftless students in my class…

Fees and tuition expenses are no excuse...

This is an institution of higher learning, not a welfare office, *Dr. So and So* cuttingly voiced.

Then there was Dr. Lesser. He preferred to be called Mister Lesser and felt violated to be referenced to anything otherwise. He was the instructor of *African American Humanities 101,* and spoke with a raspy enunciation of elocution.

(Dr. Lesser was big band jazz. His sound outdated, but nonetheless spoke an untold history loudly orchestrated. It traced its blueness of Blackness well past the dances of Congo Square and riverboats on the muddy Mississippi, veining a vascular trail from Chicago horizons to the A-train of New York. His many timbres of firm brass, opinionated woodwinds, and worldly rhythm did not dilute the countenance of the soloist wailing over the dominion.)

Recognizing the shortened temperaments of *young hearts* for our own history, he by no means rested in scolding those undergraduates watching the clock during his lectures. He

directly ridiculed and admonished students settling to be average.
Establishing an authoritarian emasculation for egos, he made
each student sing a Negro spiritual in front of the chalk-dusted
blackboard.

Swing Low, sweet cherry pies…

Wade in the bathtub…

Weave in the water children…

As each student murdered our history with wretched
voices and inaccurate lyrics, we were all excused one by one with
the infamous unsugar-coated line:

"Get out, I am not bullshiting…!"

Put out of class, I occupied my free time practicing solo
transcriptions in the silent music hall. The music hall was large
with grand vestibules, and was hauntingly quiet. The hollow
well-lit long hallways seemed as if I was the only student
interested in occupying their space.

Writing out a bebop tune with a dull pencil on
manuscript, I began to feel an eerie presence when I glanced up.
My suspicion was met by a piercing look in the window of the
practice room.

YOUNG HEARTS RUN FREE

CHAPTER V
ORIENTATION

YOUNG HEARTS RUN FREE

ENVY IS OUR BLOCKER

Orientation

A FEMININE PALE SKINNED woman made affectionate eye contact. Annoyed and challenged by her *older* white specter I grabbed my polished horn surging to the restroom to avoid her ogle. But, before the door of the stench laden tiled room closed behind me, I was followed.

Here I was excommunicated from the righteous "Afro-centric," and became crestfallen to a social cast of people known as abominations to *Blackness*. Here I hated myself for something that felt wrong, but I deemed necessary. Here I was now the conniving outcast of my family, friends, and race. Here I thought of an excuse to avoid an experiment I craved willingly, and would never reveal.

Standing at the urinal, my white professor came near with an erotic peek. I tried to hurry to finish when she stepped to my side. Looking at my penis while I shook it, she licked her lips groping my protruding bulge. Wanting to physically harm her to conceal my secret, I pretended I didn't see her.

No one has to know…

I'll do anything…

She begged.

Observing her pleated slacks, glaring diamond crusted watch, and casual shoes:

Money…

Handing me a wad of cash from a leather purse in her jacket pocket, she pulled me by my crotch into a large handicap stall.

Trying to slide the lever on the door that would not lock, she dropped to her knees kissing my *KENNETH COLE* scented bellybutton. Holding the stainless steel wall rails, she fondled the stitched zipper of my cotton jogging pants. Gnashing my teeth I asked myself: "*Why did she approach me? Do I seem that obvious?*" questioning all I knew of my virile?

Sickened to my stomach in guilt, for my cooperation she bought my books that day. I returned to the bookstore with a diminished sense of pride. A vexing turmoil pervaded me with each textbook page of western Classical theory I read in the library.

I ventured to Card after studying with the heavy backpack
and a new timepiece to pawn looking forward to falling into a
deep sleep coma. Hoping to forget my voluntary betrayal to
Black male masculinity, there I arrived only to face the very
essence of what "Black man" meant to America- Rod, the athletic
hip-hop carnal male who cared less for *whites,* and shunned
classrooms with equal distaste. Yet, he staged countless
arguments with me about his doctrine: *brother's white flight.* I
grew with envy of his *blackness* because my own mitigated
whenever he left the room.

> Hey D-town, why is your trumpet scratched and bent on
> the end?

Prying, innocently inspecting the rim of the bell.

> Where did you get this watch?

Rambling.

> None of your fuckin' business…
> Don't go through my stuff…

Angry.

Jealous.

Irritated by my unrelated irrational sacrifice of black women. I
snatched the cold instrument from him and locked it away in my
assigned closet of immoral secrecy.

> Look. I apologize...
> I was wrong for that...

I'm just a little tired from a bad day...

Cool...? I asked in regret to my only friend.

Like the other side of the pillow...

Slapping five in my hand.

After a short nap to recoup from burning the candle at both ends in making up class work, Chi-town and I set out to the dorm's gym. Hungry from our daily workout, we moved on to the crowded dining hall to eat the latest mystery meal. Sipping flat watered down beverages, I deliberately watched how the people at elongated tables ate with their napkins on their laps. I often tried to imitate their prim actions and train myself not to socialize with my mouth full, and made use of my knife.

Sometimes utensils slipped and food would fly, displaying my uncouth fringes. Disciplined manners were not necessary since my family rarely shared a meal as a group. I had to learn how to eat and speak amongst sophisticates. Haranguing the tastelessness on glass plates clinked by forks, we gazed at the sorority girls doing their obnoxious catcalls in their form fitting lettered wears.

They flirtatiously passed out tiny pink and green flyers into our trays for their latest concept for fall rush, scheduled during homecoming weekend festivities - the "Pajama Jam". In anticipation of my first college party, I frantically dug through my wardrobe eventually settling on the revealing look to show off my shapely build- white boxers, white socks, white shoes, and hat.

Playa' I got us two tickets!

This party will be off the hook!

"Aren't you going to shave before we go?" Chi-town asked as we got dressed.

I don't know how...shamed as a *man* that didn't know how to properly groom himself.

Well my *Dad* taught me...grabbing from his desk drawer a striped aerosol can of shaving cream, a bag of disposable razors, scissors, and electric barber shears.

In kinship in front of a steamed mirror he ritualistically taught me how to lather my face, shave in one direction, and trim my moustache. He plugged the clippers resonating an alerting buzz and shaped up the edges my water waved haircut. I shaved for the first time. Henceforth, I headed into *manhood* transformed from puberty.

As we walked across campus down the hill to the row of Greek houses, music could be heard blocks away. Chi-town spotted his *pick* for the night on the way there as we purposely drew attention to ourselves, flexing our cologne sprayed abs, jumping chests, and muscular arms at a girl. We went inside, and they ran to the dance floor immediately. The boxers that *told my business* didn't have pockets so the tickets, keys, and gold-foiled condoms in his hands I was left to carry. I sat on a speaker in the back of the party next to the DJ booth looking for my *black pick* of the night to show.

YOUNG HEARTS RUN FREE

CHAPTER VI

HOMECOMING

YOUNG HEARTS RUN FREE

NEGLECT IS OUR DIASTOLE

Homecoming

THE OVER POWERING SCENT of excessively sprayed
perfume, cologne, and hotness of charged hormones greeted the
air to a scene of grinding dance, wet nightgowns, and damp
silken pajama pants. Here I hid behind coupled silhouettes in
hypnotic motion to continuously thundering rhymes of indigent
poets and vibrating back beats pulsing from speakers. Packed like
sardines, movement was limited in the old house of fraternal
order whose foundation shook to the antique chandeliers.

Here I met her. Here fluttering china doe eyes and
fawning grace, she walked to me wearing a diaphanous
nightgown showing defined shoulders, and a pendant with the
stately insignia of her elite clique of sorors. Threatened by the

effulgence of her chocolate skin, I feared if I botched the proper words or riddle suitable to her modelesque sphinx, my luck would be lost. Instead she pulled my hand and without spoken word, dusk at our backs, we danced the night away as if it were our last.

Here I could care less for Monday as I tipped my all-white Yankee hat back, and swayed to contemporary melodies while being circled by Greek party hops, twirling canes, whirling mystic hand signs, and spiraling marijuana smoke. We retreated to the less compacted porch as I grabbed two condensation-misted cans from a cooler and sat on the stairs.

A semester of fond partnership began on a Friday under the stars of Alabama with "Want a *pop* umm…?", I asked with raised brow hoping to get her name.

"Kenya, and its *soda*," she answered with a *southern* response.

Briskness fell, and she asked me to hunt down her sweater. Hugging her abdomen with folded arms, my nose impressed into her soft pink and green detergent scented fleece, I marked my first glint of true affection. We could not have been greater opposites.

(*She was my Kansas City swing; I was her Cotton Club. She viewed me as a part of an exotic world encompassing criminals, guns, and unique dialect. I typecast her to a land of cozy antebellum homeliness and conservative ideals. She was the epitome of a revered southern belle. I was the metropolitan city boy to which a nation blamed its woes. She was pecan pie, chicken, and greens. I was Coney Island chili fries with cheese. Her parents and their parents flocked to HBCU. I was a first generation college student. She was of church caliber. I was all heathen. She was curvy and petite in height, yet big in confidence and soft thickness that jiggled like ripples on a pond surface. I was "red" and sculpted, but obsequious and sycophantic in nature, which contradicted my chiseled features.)*

She had a keen attraction to musicians. I liked being with a wholesome woman with her head on straight. She was a perfect *pick.* I entered the football game the next Saturday morning showing off my new *lady* on my wing.

We entered the loud stadium roaring with spectators shaking hissing black and gold pompoms. Fronted by men clad as generals, the band decked out in flaxen wool uniforms and white spats screamed an old school *Earth Wind and Fire* tune as the cymbal players rocked at its rear. Distracted from the game itself, people shuffled up and down aisles posing as runways for pretentiousness and posh outfits.

Here were the diplomatic president and first lady of HBCU. Here were the classy courted of Ms. HBCU in their sequined gowns and tuxedos. Here were the ineffective Student

Government Association cabinet members. Here were the alumni of all ages. Here were the enthusiastic tailgaters barbequing and wetting parched whistles with spirits. Here were bags of salted popcorn, roasted peanuts shells, and stale nachos with orange cheddar and spicy peppers. Here were the dueling mascots challenging each other to rally the better side. Here was the entire spectacle of spectacles with no one watching- the game on the gridiron, including Kenya and I who only surveyed each other.

In the days ahead we shed our modest goose bumps as we progressed to complete openness physically and emotionally, becoming nymphs of nuzzle and growing together. She taught me how to love a woman in the right *spot*, and how to be as gentle as I could be aggressive when the time was right. I taught her how to be free from care, and embrace sex to be *naturally* and *orally* pleasurable. Each unknown nook and cranny of campus was our hiding to spontaneously *make out* or have *a quickie*, until we ran out of places to study *Tantra*.

We equally absorbed as much warmth from each other in the weeks after our paths crossed. It was as if we were bonded at the hip, as when we were away from each other everyone questioned, "Where is your other half?"

Soon I found myself carrying her books to class in the day, and at night falling asleep clinging the phone, as neither one of us wanted to be the first to say goodnight. Chi-town often disappeared after our workouts and rarely frequented the room, which provided plenty of time to get close in *conversation* when she wore *surprises* for me. When I got my regular playing gig at the *Dive Club* she would come to egg on the support of a true fan. She would knot my neckties in the green room the way she helped father with his before work, and sit front and center, staying until the house lights came up. She was a perfect *pick*.

CHAPTER VII
STUDY HALL

ANXIETY SNIPS OUR STRINGS

Study Hall

PASS THE *DIVE CLUB'S* green room double doors I
escorted Kenya to her stage abutting observatory. My piano,
bass, and drums combo surrounded a grand Steinway catty
cornering a stained mahogany floor paneled platform.
Approaching the mic stand, I dappered a wool threaded
pinstriped navy suit and Windsor knot tie matching my lady's
shimmer.

Amidst tiered crowded seats, dim track lights back
dropped the ceiling kaleidoscoping as nightfall constellations. I
announced the title- "In a Sentimental Mood". Harmony flowered
from fingers cupped to the eighty-eight keyed contraption,
tickling rich Ellingtonian chords. While animating felt hammers

against coiled wires singing under the exposed tilted hood, a thumping upright bass and sizzling drum brushes entered.

Here I translated inner passions seducing her eardrums using a trumpet Harmon. Here I lamented delicate lullabies of cathartic savor using three brass valves, two lifetimes of aged maturity, and one blue soul. Here she fell in *love* with me sultrily gazed, rocking head, and soul melting revealing myself to have the depth of an iceberg.

After the club emptied the wait staff commenced gathering the drained brandy snifters, pilsners, and salt-rimed martini glasses. Flipping the hinging cover over the ivory, I counted out well-deserved *bread* amongst musicians and tried to hail a cab for my date. A drizzle off the club entrance eave spotted her turquoise dress when I wrapped my trench around her sleek swan, offering my hankie.

Why were you named Heart?

Intrigued outside in the thick humid air.

My mother always said that I was born a free spirit and nothing could halt the rhythm of my beating heart...

Of these three months you never spoke of your father or talked of home or old girlfriends...

Why?

Sitting on an uncushioned bench next to me.

You came to hear my set tonight...

That ballad was for you…

Changing the subject.

Talk to me baby…

Not blinking.

Did you like it?

You look *good* tonight…

Ignoring her question.

Her mood grew with impatience, as I did not answer.

Hesitating.

I did something bad…

Very bad…

Can I just be happy and *love* you?

Pulling the mute from my hand, looking away she turned concealing watering tears from her devouring stare. She pulled closer resting her head and the steel mute stuffed with linen handkerchief on my chest in solemn comfort as the cab pulled to the curb.

"*I love you too...*

Ecstatic. Getting up for her ride.

Hey, my parents are visiting from Atlanta. I want you to meet them before I go home for Thanksgiving…

Nervous as ever at the commitment, I lifted the dingy door latch.

Sure I'll meet them, but only if you come to the *Dive Club* again in that blue dress...

Deal…?

Motioning to kiss her.

Deal…

You better go back inside, it's really starting to rain

hard…

Cheesing.

I passed fare in the yellow taxi's front window and stood with
my loosened tie fluttering as they sped off.

Love?

I spoke aloud.

When she said "love", to me I thought it to be an
immature prerogative notion only for the *insane*. It was an
uncontrolled prehensile of *madness* enabling judgment to blur for
the sake of latching to dependency. I was attracted to the benefits
of her love- regular elation of spastic orgasms, counsel in
confidence, and a *cover* beauty on my arm. However, I was not
interested in submitting my wings to the mouth of a Venus
flytrap; for with the beatitudes came massive cost.

I would have to be responsible. Monogamous.
Straightfoward. Obligated. A man. The bawdiness of my *double-
sided* deviancy was too great for a *pick* to understand, and did not
care to be domestic with a female who was encroaching *insanity*.

As abruptly as I fell for her, I no longer yearned for Kenya, as she became a passing fancy associated with that word- *love.*

Love…

Love…

Love…

Love…

LOVE? The word alone became an indelible fixation repeating itself until I avoided the prospect of love completely with fear and cowardly panic.

To prove I was insouciant to the *realness of love,* I went to play some *fake contemporary jazz. (Fake jazz was sex to me. True jazz was the collective exchange of souls vertically and harmonically moving to produce climaxing improvisation. Fake Jazz has been sanitized of its dance, comedy, and sexual roots by exaggerated entertainment value, stripping itself of true sentimentality.*

Fake Jazz was a dead beat. It has become a false classroom lesson in history that is viewed with little application relative to our daily lives. It abandoned artful descriptions of universal human nature and lost its luster to the mature because it ostracizes and fails to address the expressions of blueness in Blackness anymore. Instead it engrosses culturally assimilated myths of post 52nd Street and patronized concert halls,

separating itself from roots of True Jazz: black, sensuous,
raggedy, funky, swinging, ghetto, romantic music. True jazz was
love.)

The *dead weight* of my parricide was reincarnating itself
on my back, and slowly I morphed into someone I hated- my
father. I was going to prove that no declaration of *real love* was
going to handle me on this holiday. I *ran* back in the bar and
called my *fake* woman to pick me up.

She was the new White *pick* on the side from a place
called *Cloverdale*- a neighborhood of *old* money across the tracks
dividing Montgomery by race. She did all of the nasty things I
would never ask my *girlfriend* to do. Serving as company on the
weekends when the in-state students deserted campus, she was
the misogynistic *hustle* that gave me money to strip when the
Dive was booked. She was my *Sally*, as I was her *Thomas
Jefferson*. She was just an experimental *pick* catering to my
immature ego when she told me "How big it was…" and "How
good it was…".

On a dressing room vanity circled by *Hollywood* round
light bulbs flickering, I lowered a pink thong down her creamy
white legs. With underwear at mid thigh I bent her over. Digging
painted nails into my skin I lifted her to the counter, as thunder
erupted outside like cannons.

Hustling without a charming kiss, my fingers tangled in her blond hair, I pushed as she shrieked my name until the materialization of *love* dissipated under flashes of lightning. "Get off of my daughter!" a voice murmured like a plunger on a trombone.

It had to be poetic justice for my bad deeds. There behind us in the dressing room stood a ragging freckle-faced woman, soaked by rainwater and holding a pistol.

Get the hell out of here before I blow your ass away…
It was my professor from the restroom!
It was the woman whose watch my new girlfriend was wearing!
Daughter? Mother and daughter too?

As if she had seen a ghost, she stood speechless, lowering the gun as I tipped out of the door holding my belt loops *running*.

YOUNG HEARTS RUN FREE

CHAPTER VIII
MIDTERMS

YOUNG HEARTS RUN FREE

FEAR IS OUR CLOGGING PLIGHT

Midterms

I *RAN* AND I *ran* and I *ran*. *I ran just as my father had run*. I *ran* hoping I wouldn't feel a bullet pierce my back. I *ran* thinking of what I would say when I picked up the phone as soon as I arrived home. Perhaps I would say, "Hey Kenya, *I love you too*," just to have someone to *run* to, although I couldn't truly love her because she was *just* a *cover pick* that gave good *conversation*.

Here, I knew it to be an extensive night. Here, clouds typically footprinting the sky, quickly pushed past leafless clapping swaying branches. Here, the rain moved so fast it misted a hailing spray. Here, winds howled through cracks of houses,

and the once picturesque landscape became a darkened day.
Here, people made a mass exodus from stores and shops taking
refuge in their homes, and noise from expressway traffic hovered
over the waning mêlée. Here I ran.

Exhausted and now resolved to sticking to the stationary
insanity of *love*, I *ran* thinking how it feels to be alone for the
holiday. I *ran* all the way back to the ransacked stairwell of Card
littered with jock straps, crew cut socks, and smelled of
mentholated therapy rub. Coming from the opposite direction,
two police officers drew near.

In retreating, again I took flight from the campus dorm
into the lessening rain. Roses and lit signs shaped as "*H*"
decorated the grounds for the festive holiday. Oak leaves foliaged
and snowed in Thanksgiving harvest, rolling about the wet
walkways. Luckily unscathed by harms way, in the mill factory
scented fog I now *ran* from police when I stumbled upon Chi-
town.

Passing the monolithic stone monument that read:
"HBCU FOUNDED 1867"

Bordered by

"HBCU"

in green shrubbery, he walked in a procession between a channel of hooded figures yielding wood paddles, chanting like entranced shaman knighting their shoulders. Now his circumstance became clear, and it made logical sense. Rod chose to pledge this semester.

I often wondered why he rarely sustained free time. Perhaps he was at basketball practice, but it was football season. Perhaps he had a job occupying his time, but his mom sent funds every month. Perhaps he had a steady girlfriend, but *we* had sex with a new *pick* every weekend.

He now reined membership to one of the many casts of separate but equal social divisions at HBCU:

(My first lesson of acclimation was the cast system of college bands:

There was the cast of haves and have-nots. These were students receiving financial aid and those who were not eligible.

There was the regional cast. This was the division of the slow talking country folks and militant city individuals.

There was the political cast. These were opinionated enthusiast and those who squandered their votes.

There was the hue cast. These were those who were separated by the degree of melanin in their skin.

There was the academic cast. These were those who are separated by students of culture and those who only attended college because their parents forced them.

There was the legacy cast. These were those whose parents attended HBCU and those who were novices for their namesake.

And, then there was the power cast- i.e. athletes and Greeks. It was a prevailing title that was a double-edged sword. The compensation was reception into the community of brotherhood, but it had a high price of glory.

These were those men who often were forced to squander academics and money, but excelled in stature because of their ability to withstand hazing- the systematic process of creating a 21st century slave to serve the master of amalgamated ways of thinking and composite gestures of imitation.) He was now a greenhorn in Pan Hellenic Elysium.

Hey D-town. Nigga I'm Greek BABY!

We're heading back to the room to celebrate with some yak (cognac) and snacks. Come on man, let's go…

Overjoyed, he pulled me back towards Card Hall that was then circled by at least ten siren police cars with strobing lights.

I was going to jail! I thought. *This was it. It had to be poetic justice for my bad deeds. I was going to jail for killing my father.* My heart was thumping.

Just when I expected to go into the dorm, we detoured to the car of one of his brothers. Passing me a strawberry Swisher filled with a fragrant potion of *sticky-icky* moistened on its *peace pipe* tip, my paranoia deteriorated.

We have to hit the store first...

Are you okay? (Coughing)

Sensing my apprehension.

I'm...

(ssssst)

Cool...

Nik...ka...(choking)

Like the other side of the pillow nigga? He laughed.

Nigga I'm tight like gnat booty... Joking and toking.

We exchanged *riffs* all the way to the liquor store. We drove in the tattered car knocking and *smoking* to a shanty with no name on its billboard. Met by the acquaintances of beggars pleading their cases for spare change and alcohol, we interjected guiltlessly passing them to "Well-God-bless-you-then's" and "Can-you's". Inside I added to my mounting credit card debt by buying the items of everyone's choice.

The clerk did not ask any of us for an ID, and we did not encourage him. Incoming to our return to Card, the rings of the bottle lids ticked. We gulped with faded eyes before parallel parking in an oil stained slant.

I was going to jail! I thought, forgetting Chi-*town's fortune. This was it. It had to be poetic justice for my bad deeds* (cough). *I was going to jail for killing my father.* My heart was thumping as I tipped the bottle high. *I was going to jail! This was it. It had to be poetic justice for my bad deeds. I was going to jail for killing my father…*(ssst)

In a pink polo shirt, treading quickly towards the parking lot was the white girl and her mother- my experimental bathroom *pick.* Behind them was a man with the texture of hair always appearing wet, and distinct olive skin making him look like a glowworm.

How could you fuck me and my daughter?

I loved you…

I was willing to leave my family for you…

I wanted to be with you…

My face sank to the ground as they outted my lustful secret to my roommate and his pack. Chi-town stared at me as if I had leprosy.

"Hi are you the son of a bitch that's fucking my wife," the man said, directing his angry comment at Rod.

"You got me fucked up with somebody else dog," Chi-town yelled.

Do we know you playa'?

"Don't get that ass beat fag"…the crew of intoxicated fellows threatened. My knees began to knock as my intuition told me to hit him with the liquor bottle, but Chi-town sucker punched him *first*. In a barrage of kicks and stomps, the man covered his head falling to the ground. In the confusion he pulled his pistol and pointed it at me. Chi-town and his brothers fled towards the dorm, leaving me there. He got up.

WAP!

He hit me across the side of my ear with the cartridged butt of the gun. Forcing the hard barrel to my jugular:

You motherfucka'…

WAP!

Mad. WAP! WAP! WAP! WAP!

Stop, I love him…

Softer. Sincere.

I loved you…

Bloody faced. Monotone.

Do you love her?

You don't love me. You love my dick…

Is that what you want? Right…

Huh? Isn't it?

Pulling *it*.

Is that what you want to shoot me for?

A squad car passed us and he hid the gun in his pocket.

Are you okay?

Yes sir…

Well you fellas' need to get inside…

There has been a hate crime reported on campus….

A murder…

Running to the dorm.

CHAPTER IX
FINAL EXAMS

TRUTH IS OUR ACHE

Final Exams

ON THIS DAY, I journeyed the fraternal rite of passage
every Black man in due course travels, but seldom deserves to
cross its burning sands- the day his morale as an American is
permanently tarnished. I never mourned a soul until that day; not
even my father. Naïve to the strength of speech, I never knew
what it meant to be privileged to wear rose-colored glasses. I
never knew consequences for the nonchalant usage of the word
nigga until that day.

Here, the magnitude of potential light dimmed by the
teachings of William Lynch. Here, the finale' of an incomplete
symphony rested on its leading tone. Here, a prince was

dethroned of a guaranteed crown of inalienable rights. Here hung the body of Mr. Greathouse.

The stairwell was spray painted with misspelled obscenities, and swaying from the rafters like a pendulum on a grandfather clock was the martyr of nonce. His cut neck was stretched open and his clothes dripped of his assailants' urine.

In our *inebriation* we observed in horror, as we all felt dehumanized at the dorm director's debasement. Largely something that could only be in a black and white documentary or old sepia photo, the rebirth of history on that banister saliently produced an account in blaring color to the *young hearts* in the hall that day.

The dark underbelly of the South's racism hit with *sobering* resiliency. We thought that it was buried with Wallace and extinguished by Rosa's smile of triumph. We heard Handy's blues before and saw the bomb craters on King's porch not far from campus. We saw the cotton bulbs sprouting from our ancestor's graves and discussed the future of the nation with Dr. Cornell West. But on this day, the South made us contemplate a *sobering truth.*

Two men were arrested. Their breach of life was fueled by *rage* stemming from the actions of Mr. Greathouse's *dead weight*- his *son* who was accused of murdering a white cop. In retaliation they made an example of his father.

(Chewing tobacco dripping from their mandibles, they waited for a response in the rain after busting a window, as if they had thrown breadcrumbs for unsuspecting prey to follow. Startled, the man emerged to investigate in the storm; his brandisher held a flannel shirt over his gray head while the other tied a noose. The elderly man was fiercely dragged up the stairs by rope, tied to the balcony, and swiftly dropped, snapping his neck like a twig. In their effort to flee, the students restrained the two men until officials arrived. "One less nigger!" they shouted from the rear of a squad car.)

The moment was bittersweet. In the misfortunate calamity I was relieved I wasn't the culprit the police hunted. I was still free of my *dead weight*. But, the dire loss of a *living* testament to the will of Black men was immensely *sorrowful*. The *young hearts* of the dorm and I were forever besmirched by the undying will of *raging* hatred for our cloaks of dark hue.

The rain subsided. Mosquitoes stung my forearms, as I waited in the courtyard for the investigators to wheel the sheeted stretcher to the ambulance. Through the cockroaches scattering like spilled marbles across the pavement, I cunningly walked to the opposing stairwell where there were no police.

Lying alone on my back, I stared at my room ceiling counting the multicolored layers of paint flaking back, wondering how many other *hearts* laid in this place. (*In this spot I asked myself: What is a son's obligation to his father? It should be his intent to devote a lifetime of labor and toil to the fields of legacy.*

Sons who till the soil of enlightenment with cultural awareness, dedication to the homestead, and delineation from bleak motivation to do great things must weed the regeneration of "dead beat sons" out of the field of trite sensibilities. Despite the inexcusable lack of effort on the part of shallow men shifting the burden of responsibility of manhood to boys, sons of the dead must make it a necessity to be free- become educated, brilliantly mindful of their history, and boldly seen in the eyes of their children. We are obligated to nurture our seeds to fruitful beings that will feed the hearts and minds of their children. We are indeed obligated to live for the growth of our crop.)

Here I realized my mother lived a lifetime for me. It was a daunting task as I relived the last moments of my life and recognized my vain. I was finally at the advent of *adulthood*. Looking in retrospect I wondered how she did it. How did she make it to an age of nirvana without ever showing a slight symptom of regret, distain, or weakness? Remembering my mother's concern for my well being, with my southpaw shaking of nervousness from the sight of seeing death *again*, I wrote a letter home.

Dear Mom:

Happy Thanksgiving. It has been a while since we last spoke. It would be good to hear your voice and have some homemade turkey. I hope that life is improving as I pray for you and the family to have a good holiday. It has been a tough year; try daily and be strong, I am proud of you.

As for my well being, I am good. I am spending my time studying. I have been exposed to people from all over the globe and I am taking college in stride. I beg God for direction and guidance; maybe he will hear me one day soon.

The days of the Southern Indian summer were long and heated, but kind smiles often made me forget about degrees. I still miss the downtown festivals at Hart Plaza and the breeze off of the Detroit River on a nice evening. Sometimes I daydream about running through the huge steal fountain, and looking up to see you smiling across the crowd. Better yet, waiting all night to see the fireworks on the Fourth of July, just to fall asleep at the first blast.

I have a feeling that good things will come about with nineteen. Know that I am safe and doing my best to change. I love you.

Your Son,

Heart

PS- Forgive me for not responsibly saying thank you for your strength!

When I saw the lynched body, I was reminded of how I left home in a hurry. I remembered her sacrifice for me. I remembered my graduation six months before. It was all vividly coming back.

CHAPTER X
GRADUATION

ANGER IS OUR ARRHYTHMIA

Graduation

WHAT IS A DEADBEAT dad? Is he in truth a dad or just a *dead weight* truly beating feeble shoulders to exhaustion with his dogmatic claim to the term? In his folly he forfeits fatherhood leaving in his trail of *abandonment* a sullen *seed* of resentment in the beating *heart* of his child.

A copulated conception of his cower, I was left to navigate a confusing world with little guidance or protection. In consequence of his retribution, I was penalized to a childhood fixed in incessant resolute impediment. What was his motive? What could have been the x-factor incentive to cast me into an existence with the brand of insignificance?

Here it was the inoculation of conscience and relinquished *responsibility* to family allegiance. Here his false immunity never was, and the arrhythmia of unseen potential took its toll on the aorta of his son- *Heart,* so my mother named me. Here I was the abnormal *abandoned* proliferation of my mother's statutory rape, graduating from high school.

The night before the big day my mother and I went to dinner. She splurged on the best restaurant in *Greektown-* a small ethnic village adjacent to downtown Detroit.

"Can you afford this place?" I asked concerned looking at the menu.

"Gotdammit' I can buy my only child a meal on the biggest day of his life. Get anything you want," upset at my audacity.

In the eatery gilded in Parthenon columns and hand painted frescos of fattened women, we ordered lamb stuffed grape leaves. "OPA!" the waiter screamed as he flambéed a cheese appetizer flashing next to the table topped with white doilies. Sipping her wine she spoke:

Your *father* came to see me. I told him about your
graduation tomorrow…
Was it ok to invite him?
With a sudden loss of appetite
No…

You should have asked…

I excused myself not touching my food and left without looking back.

Heart, wait…

You don't understand…

I *ran* and lingered at the bus stop until a pair of lights with "WOODWARD AVE" above them appeared. I gave the driver a handful of wrinkled singles and coins. Irate, I sat in the back riding up and down the rows of dilapidated buildings until the sun came up. When the driver yelled, "Hey kid, my shift is over" I walked home tired and rattled my key in the door.

SLAP!

Where in the…

SLAP!

Hell…

SLAP!

Have you…

SLAP! SLAP!

Been?

I have looked all over this city for you…

Panicked.

Not speaking, with a red face I walked past her and pulled my robe and tasseled hat off a hanger in the linen closet. I hit the shower, dressed, and still did not utter a word to her on the way out.

We drove to the school on a beautiful spring day in early June in *angry* silence. I lined up with the massive crowd of parading beings, bearing strides of optimism and smiles filled with spirit. During the entire ceremony I contemplated what led to this day.

When I should have been thinking of new opportunity and adulthood, instead I pictured the many years my mother and I struggled. I saw when my mother sold her body and soul so I could have a coat when I walked in the exposing snow to school. I pictured when we spent holidays at a shelter with strange people on cots or when we were evicted, holiday cheer no longer twinkled in our eyes. I remembered sleeping on blankets on cold floors of unfamiliar places or when there were no blankets at all. I remembered the times when we didn't have heat in the harsh winters of Michigan.

I visualized the times when we ate potatoes tasting like the kerosene heaters on which we cooked or when there was nothing to share at all. I recalled taking cold baths or when there was no water. I remembered the days we didn't have electricity I read in the dark by candlelight or when there were no candles to burn.

As I walked to my diploma rolled in the principal's hand, I saw him over the applause. He wore a modest suit and a slight smirk. He looked like a distant relative I recognized, but failed to place a name. He passed a hard-shelled case to my mother and exited the back of the unventilated gym.

The seniors threw their mortars into the air in joy as I sat distracted. When the ceremony ended my mother handed me a silver trumpet with inlaid pearl valve caps incased by a suede-lined trunk.

This is from your *father*…

He wanted to wish you well with your music scholarship to college…

Will you meet him?

In fuming *anger* with my lips balled I demanded:

Where is he? I have something to return to him…

Snatching the instrument while speaking the first words I had spoken since the day before.

He will be at this address at six o'clock tonight…

Giving me a white Hallmark envelope with a motel address scribbled on its corner.

I left from the school still wearing my black robe. Marching to his parking lot doorstep with the caseless horn in my hand I forcefully banged and waited, pacing in repetition for him to answer. When the door creaked, I tossed the envelope at his feet. He knelt to pick it up when in anticipation I lifted the weapon.

CHAPTER XI

LETTER

OF

ACCEPTANCE

YOUNG HEARTS RUN FREE

DEAD WEIGHT IS OUR INFARCTION

Letter Of Acceptance

I WAS NOT PERPETUALLY striking my father's head with my *empty* trumpet. Metaphorically I was casting blows of retribution to every day my soul burned defenselessly in an unrelenting world of clutched purses and veiled criticisms. I crushed the skull of pessimism shackling my ankles to an anchor inside the pit of eternal bastardization. I cut the throats of voices bellowing *criminal* euphemisms and *nigger*. With *rage* I exposed the brain of the rabid mongrel as some eyes in pale faces regarded *me*.

Here I belligerently wept in *sorrow* as I indirectly murdered the half of myself I rarely saw or controlled, but always carried its burden on my back. Here I stood to get the *dead weight* off I no longer mourned or played dirges in B-flat to. Here my core boiled in sobbing isolation with an invisible man I hated. Notwithstanding the possibility that he too hated me, I killed in self-defense as he strangled me with an umbilical cord of a stymied chance from birth.

Incredulously I struck in inexorable madness until a splash of blood spattered my cheek. He did not scream in agony or wrench in shock. With a single backward step with the flesh of his forehead butterflied open, he slid down the wall behind leaving a trailed smear from his coarse sliced scalp. The silver horn with chips of bone and blood on the dented bell gonged to the ground as I froze in disbelief.

Cautiously I closed the door and knelt to my father's last breath whispering, "Forgive me" in my ear. Shocked, I quivered in insurmountable regret as I held back a welling lump in my esophagus. He looked directly in my eyes when his pupils drew inward and neck went limp. His corpse fell to the side like a jack-in-the-box, as rivers of still warm blood oozed down his cranium.

Not flinching, I sat in *sorrow*. Time was our foe and it won. I never got to say to him, "I forgive you". I never got to say, "I need you". Slipping my palm down the lids of his eyes, I held my father for the first and last time as he lay with the peace of lifeless still.

Spent, I looked at his face for the *first* time with the wonder of a newborn seeing resemblance of myself. I had his distinguished nose and lips. Our irises were the same shade of auburn. We had the same birthmark on our necks.

Rage filled my heart again. I walked to a fading mirror attached to the his-and-her sinks, scratching my face as if I were trying to rip it off. I grabbed a pair scissors on the end of the counter and began to cut; I cut *his* thick eyebrows from *my* face; I cut *his* curled lashes. I cut off the dead weight of *myself* I always hated, but did not see until this day.

In solitude, baptized in my father's gore I reached for the envelope under his right index. Peeling out the greeting card immersed in blood and folded at its midpoint, I opened it and recited its passages. In bold letters printed to the left there was, "HAPPY GRADUATION!" and to the right in hand written script, "Run free young Heart. Run free". I have been running ever since.

Chapter XII

Financial Aid

YOUNG HEARTS RUN FREE

GREED IS OUR MURMUR

Financial Aid

MY FATHER WAS A killer. When he asked "Dear father what shall be my legacy?" my grandfather's response: *Give a man a fish, and he eats for a day; hook a man like a fish, and we'll eat for a lifetime.* His inheritance was an order of survival in fighting an uphill battle of a long string of tarnished legacies. My father was a generational drug dealer.

Here, schooling his offspring to measure, roll, and count eight balls, mescaline, and dime bags before kindergarten, they made others sell for him by high school. Here, Grandfather never instructed him on the basic keys to life, but professed a legacy of teachings to smuggle and sell so well, his best customer was his own son.   Here, systematically deteriorating he evolved into a creature whose cravings made him steal for *the product.*

He begged. He cried. He stole. Not supporting the household and denying benefits gave salivating leverage to bite his piercing fangs into a rotten flesh stench laden with disgraceful defect. A welling primitive urge often diluted bloodshot eyes and lips pasting with dehydration, primally devouring his homestead on a skewer of hollow narcotics supplied by close relatives.

Steering me from an evil inheritance by moving and dodging, working petty jobs paying very little, money wasn't plentiful, as I often blamed my mother for our unhappy strife. Shielding me from a life she knew internally was not for me, because it made my potential unseen, my future was sheltered from disillusion by temporary financial aid in exchange for my soul. Yet, coveting what I lacked, my friends sported new shoes; my shoes bore grimy tongues. My friends modeled new school haberdashery; my underwear beamed with holes. My friends grubbed three meals a day; my meals were dined exclusively at school.

She didn't decide to forfeit that legacy until Christmas before my first year of life. They bought the biggest spruce in the lot. Shopping for so many ornaments that the tree sagged in glittery yuletide repose, he and my mother spent all of the eve

cooking to the sound of the *Temptations'* "This Christmas"
replaying in the stereo tape player.

   She sat and waited for him to join the table draped in
turkey, dressing, macaroni, cinnamon dusted yams, hot greens,
chitlins', and sweet potato pie. She waited. She waited two hours.
After the three hundred and fiftieth "Hang all the mistletoe…"
She was furious.

   Kicking open the unhinged bathroom door, slumped
wide-eyed flicking a Bic in a haze of smoke there he lay.
Slapping the scalding pipe to the floor, grabbing him by the
collar she gave the best present one could offer- a six-month trip
to the Wayne County Rehab Center. An unexpected gift arrived
as my father dropped off the face of the earth filled with his own
poison: a son. While he was getting *clean,* she was devising our
own escape from her prison- my father.

   Instead of asking for *forgiveness* when my mother visited
the rehab center before release, he asked that she drop off a
shipment in a case, wanting to set up shop and bring in new
customers to recoup losses while away. When the time came to
pick up my father in June from the program, digging in a dented
blue *Folders* coffee can underneath the squeaking floor boards
behind the rusted cold steel kitchen stove, she took all of the
money saved from his murderous enterprise and moved;
Preoccupied with being top neighborhood salesman under the

binding employee contract of addiction, again and again it remained *his* parent. It told *him* when it was bedtime. It told *him* when to awake. It told him when it was time for church- meanwhile he worshiped a glass stuffed with drugs as his family left.

Wanting to apologize, he asked for *exoneration* seventeen years later, explaining his pride that I wasn't making the same mistakes. That is what my mother attempted to tell me at dinner when I stormed off. Unfortunately, I killed in haste before his epiphany heralded.

Lifting my head from the greeting card the night of his death, in the shadows of the door stood my mother. "Dear God! Dear God… What did you do?" she said falling to her knees as if to pray. Unable to answer, I turned in dishonor ashamed I made her suffer the indignity of a murderous son.

We didn't speak as we wrapped him in a paisley quilt and put him in the trunk of her old Buick. Scrubbing the room, we cleaned it of its soils and returned the key to the desk clerk. In the obscurity of night with bleached bloodied fingernails we drove to the closed *Boblo Park* boat docks, and tossed him over into forgotten past.

That summer his seagrape-encased wallet floated to the shores of Belle Isle. The carnivores of the Detroit River mangled his partial remains past recognition. The forensic department traced his identification and cross-referenced his name to my birth certificate. When I didn't claim his remnants, a femur was placed in a pauper's field in an unmarked gravesite. Using the only gift he ever gave, I made my departure on a 747, as I was *free* of his *dead weight*. I ran *free* to enlightenment hidden in *red clay* awaiting my arrival, with a bent silver horn in my rickety hands.

After writing my mother her Thanksgiving letter from my dorm room, I wrote one to my dead father, but I wasn't ready to share my feelings. I threw the letters in my desk drawer, and went to sleep off my liquor.

Chapter XIII

Grade Report

DECEIT IS OUR THROMBOSIS

Grade Report

IN THE AMBIGUITY OF night there was a presence in
my dorm room. Creaking in the silence, a hand touched my head.
I knew it was Kenya; I felt that touch before. Kisses patted my
sideburns, pillowing to my lips. Sensuously putting her mouth
over mines, kissing upside-down our tongues twirled: first
lightly, then deeply. Alternating lips from top to bottom, bottom
to top we exchanged *I Love you's* in nervous mouthfuls of air.

I love you too..." nonchalantly saying so to get what I
craved. Smacking and twisting our heads, breathing hard in
anticipation that some uncanny fellow freshmen might hear, or
perhaps Rod might rambunctiously twist his basketball calloused

hands on the knob without fair warning. With left hand holding the top of my head, and right hand pulling up my shirt, I felt her rubbing and feeling my washboard tight from my daily workouts. Up and down her now warm hands were tucking my shirt overhead; Licking each nipple, flicking the right, and pinching the left.

Maneuvering my long imprint squeezing my favorite red athletic shorts, revealing a pulsing triangular head, my rough tickling palms pushed her back.

Wait...

I commanded.

We need a condom...

Shh...

Hushing me by pulling *it* out of its meaty fold, forcing up a clear glaze, time stopped as she took my gland fist to fist touching the back of her throat. Every nerve ending electrified as she stretched *it,* slurping like a melting Popsicle. My eyes rolled and swirled as she slapped *its* heaviness on her face, vacuuming, sniffing, gagging, and tapping each cheek. She could only go half way, but that didn't stop her from trying.

Both at a time pulling her pants down, exposing her lace I decided to return the favor. Tightening on my middle dexterity, fingering deep inside of her softness, her hairless legs quivered. I noticed her flower smell as I felt up her smooth tall sleekly muscular thighs running up to a small petite frame. Impulsively tonguing her crevice, bending over my face her back arched in howling wet sweetness. The dark room filled with heat as I licked, tensing her deeper into an ecstasy that she initiated.

"Did you lock the door"...

"Quiet"...

Cutting off my air with her brown body, she sank on my watering tongue in a spread. Gumming, smelling, quaffing on my nose, glazing with my spit, her tightness loosened as her arm pulled me harder into her hips, riding in lip biting wetness.

Walking her backwards, pushing to the teetering desk I straddled her long legs, bending them as she sank onto my big thickness. Filling her cavity forward inch by inch, stretching past her limits, we sea-sawed each other, bobbing with urgency knowing that my roommate was not far. The rocking desk squeaked.

Gym shoes shuffled under the beams of a shadowed rectangle where curious ears pressed their way. Snickers and jeers became omnipresent as echoes of our fervor became rampantly obvious. Doing a 180 turn, leading me to the sounds she cautiously stood on the balls of her feet. Holding her mouth and kissing her tense shoulders, immaturely I had no mercy pushing her face to the cold paint.

Burying her head down, I sank my *knife* in like a baker cutting a cake with ease, pressing her navel flat against the loudly rattling dorm room door. Turning to face me, we kissed on our wall of exhibitionism gasping for air. Humming and moaning, wiggling youthfully breast to breast our hearts patting out of our chests.

"Oh God..."

"Ahh"…

"ssst"…

"Does it hurt?"…

"Ohh it hurts so good"…

Shivering in slippery detached pleasure, shoving without warning her intestines tightened, rising in sweaty exhaustion. Slapping down harder, with chest pecks jumping, my biceps flexed as I punched until I had no more control. With forehead caressing her Adam's apple, she pulled my shirt nearer, choking me to throbbing shots of elation.

Marinating inside embraced arms, we died in each other's laps drained, firing in stringy passion strokes as if it were our first time erupting. My white *Cloverdale pick* had deceived me. Patting until the last burst of unprotected syrupy juice fell, the door swung light in, as we continued suctioned in ridicule.

"We had to finish were we left off"...

Stepping out the room

"Keep this between me and you alright"…

Index finger to my lips.

"Shh, my dad is going to kill me"…

I knew this would be the end of my relationship with Kenya, as word traveled fast amongst the bellowing gossipers who reported the campus dish like paperboys pronouncing the latest selling scandalous headline. Squirming through the dank hall's whispers, I scurried to the shower as Rod sat to watch a movie intentionally ignoring my presence.

"Cool"…

I asked with a devious smirk.

"Naw' man, never"…

"Hell naw'"…

"Why?"

"What the fuck!"

Chi-town I'm just doing what whites have done to brothas' fo' years: fuck em'…

Leaving…

"Hell naw'"…

"Goodnight"…

"You are still drunk"…

He returned five seconds later with an equally devious grin.

"Oh, you scared me for a minute"…

"Next time I fight for your lady, she betta' bring her mother for me"…

"You know it "…

CHAPTER XIV

End of the Semester

YOUNG HEARTS RUN FREE

GROWTH IS OUR BURDEN

End of the Semester

THROWING CAUTION TO THE wind upon Mr.
Greathouse's death, being pistol-whipped and chased, I realized
life was not guaranteed on any given day. Kenya looked to me
with a new optimism in our *friendship*, and I dreamed of a
lifestyle I knew possible, but never imagined befitted me. After
my shower I was knocked out from my alcohol.

Alabama skies rarely revealed their stars until I met
Kenya's *friendship*. Mustering nerve after my nap, I called my
pick to express what I thought she expected me to say, afraid to
tell her I couldn't love her. Speaking softly not interrupting Chi-
town's deep hog call slumber:

Babe, I love you...

Heart…I am pregnant…

Stunned.

Taken back.

Are you sure?

Serious.

Yes I'm sure…

Someone is on the phone…

I'll call you back.

Click.

Here I felt some indescribable entity tensing under my rib cage I thought to be breaking my chest open. Here a chance is given to redeem my wrongs by raising a child providing things my own father seldom comprised. Here I was young, by no means wealthy, but retained plenty of love. It took me a while to gather my senses and settle into bed when she failed to call back immediately.

Ringing in the silence...

Let's be honest, neither one of us is ready for love or a kid…

Maybe we shouldn't see each other anymore…

Murmuring in a heartbroken tone.

Why? I'm not good enough for you...

And the baby?

Mad.

126

Tell that White BITCH to have your baby...

Betta' yet, tell her husband…

Click!

Calling her back.

Wait don't hang up…

Is it true?

What?

Is it true?

My girlfriend called me up tonight, and said that you and

this girl be hookin' up regularly…

Is it you?

That's all I wanna' know…

No…

Un huh. Well is there anyone else?

Deep Breath.

Okay, to tell you the truth…

Well see what had happened was…

There was this White girl and…

Cutting me off.

White?

A White bitch? A White BITCH!

Click.

Calling her back.

Don't call here no mo' punk ass bitch…

I know about everything…

I'm glad I'm killing yo' baby…

And *my brothers* are gonna' fuhg' you UP!

Click.

Calling back.

Please don't end it like this…

I'm sorry…

Whateva', dat white girl will get dat ass wooped…

Aight' den'…

You'll miss dis'…

Please…

It wasn't big enough for me anyway…

Dat itty-bitty thing drowns in my shit…

Click

After the barrage of my unreturned insults, she later called screaming. Rushing to the hospital, droplets spotted the triage couch beneath her. Holding a barely swollen stomach huffing and puffing, she was wheelchair pushed by a nurse down a maternity ward. She drifted off. Hours I waited in the hospital lobby holding Chi-town's attention, as he donned his new Greek paraphernalia.

Tossing and turning on the small wood furniture, I drifted off into a dream tranced in nightmare vignettes.

Cradled in the fetal position, draped in Kenya's beautiful walnut skin, a tiny boy curled bearing my looks. Miniature fingers and toes wiggling, with closed lids he whimpered. Gripped, I pictured my father's seaweed enveloped rotting body standing over the prematurely born infant, squeezing his teeny neck choking him with his own umbilical cord.

I awoke sweating. Breaking from my brief sleep, I sprang from the makeshift bed yelling, "Something is wrong". Restrained by Chi town, he gave me the bad news. "The baby was breached when she fought that white girl, and was... I'm sorry man…but…she was bleeding…and." My child was dead. My son was unseen potential. It must have been poetic justice for my bad deeds.

The Monday after the holiday break, I still hadn't heard from Kenya, and I was still too embarrassed to face my white pick. I eventually got the chance to meet her parents, when she returned. Searching the day for her, I waited outside. Loitering at her dorm to avoid my own, the afternoon proved unproductive until a blue Lincoln parked regally. Tension was their disposition, as it radiated disapproval sighting my presence. "Is that him?" her raisin-faced mother asked turning her nose up. Palming Kenya's back, a large man with salt and peppered hair forcefully escorted her past me without allowing her to acknowledge my presence.

WEAK ASS BITCH…

NO GOOD…

CHEATING ASS…

NIGGA…

SON OF A BITCH…

LOW LIFE…

ASSHOLE…

"Stay away from my daughter", her father threatened as her mother condemned me to Hell. She must have broken the news to her parents of her pregnancy, my infidelity, and the fight. Without consulting Kenya, *they* decided it was best to not see me. And that was that- the end of my *love* affair, my child's life, and the *fall semester*. Here I realized I was more like my father than I was aware.

Our fathers abandoned us both. We both were "*dead beats*" as we used sex as a defense mechanism to underscore our deficiencies in untaught manhood like untamed Mandingoes. We both were reckless, neglecting accountability in rash gratification. We both harmed our children before they embarked the prospect of *life*. We both sought *forgiveness* when it was too late.

I needed to face my *anger* and mistakes once and for all. I needed to bring closure to my *dead weight*. I needed to grow up and accept *responsibility* for my own *life*. After final exams I set out to the Greyhound station and purchased a ticket for the next inbound bus scheduled for Detroit.

Dimly lit by the slowly descending orange sun, the road cluttered with chunks of mud rocks hitting the base of the trotting bus seemed to stretch about the dell endlessly. As the hot eye of God wilted a pungent scent from magnolia trees, the deeply crimson colored trail looked minute in comparison to the towering weeping willows gracefully bowing with spots of Spanish moss peeking through their leaves.

Peering through the dust haze covered window like a child with an oversized spyglass in hand, my consciousness digressed to another world, as cracking pecans sounded as they were pushed to the ground by light temperate gusts of wind. All that was etched in my view at that instant were all of the things that codified *South* in my lasting memory.

For it was here I became a man. It was here I fell in *love*. It was here I found my enduring passion for my musical virtuosity. Frustrated with rejection of my permanent cloak of dark hue, it was here I was introduced to *rebels* without a just cause. It was here I began to chart a course of legacy renewed for my surname.

But at that moment, my only object of interest was the peaceful consolation of cirrus clouds in an undulating marble-like sky, which helped me to escape two silent catalysts for early

death- the excessive weights of rage and sorrow. Not
withstanding the brief reminiscence of nostalgia, encamped
within the confines of the small iron coach I was on my way to
view mortality in my likeness- the grave of my father.

The affinity of a man I barely knew, I, his spitting image
would have to stand over it to come to grips; I would have to
accept that there would never be reconciliation. Time was our foe
and it won.

Despite whatever hesitant adversity I felt in my heart, I
exceeded my reservations hoping to face my demon (the lurking,
ever nudging fact that I hated an invisible man, and the
possibility that he too hated me).

The South cradled my evolution and helped me to avoid
its nuisance- a fact cultivating an incomplete *Heart* perforated
with chances untaken. Formidably, I expected this day to come,
but the notion that I would not be affected gave me a boundless
impermeable arrogance keeping me less concerned with him
succumbing to his fate. You see, I killed my father before he
killed me, and I was *free*- free to say as a *man:* "I forgive you".

At this juncture I made it home groggy and stiff from the
extensive twenty-hour trek bringing me from the basin of my
hiding place. I walked the short route to the monorail train, and
dropped the clinking tokens imprinted with the phrase *Detroit*

People Mover. "Business District," the computerized voice rang as the automated doors popped ajar.

Crossing the gantlet intersection on *Jefferson,* I proceeded to the entrance of *Hart Plaza* decorated with pearling Christmas lights matted in the trees. Greeted by floating tugboats and gray seagulls gliding in the air above, I crunched through the partially melted snow mounds buckshotted with salt. Pulling out a crinkled letter folded in the insert pocket of my *London Fog,* I began to read:

Thank you for teaching me the runs of life in death...

I learned to not run from love because I didn't know how to respond to those who loved me, but to accept the change of my consistent suspicion and distrust into taut tools of return dedication...

I learned not to run from authority, but to accept those who attempt to correct my wrongs to forsake of my own labor...

I learned not to run from education, but to accept it as visibility to those that see me as translucent...

I learned not to run from the past, but to accept it as a harbor of enduring strength and a school of streetwise savvy...

*I learned not to run from my hue, but to accept it as a
bronze of understanding that in the blueness of Blackness
joy is made so much sweeter…*
*I learned not to run from women, but to accept their
intellect as a complement to my conscientiousness…*
*I learned not to run from family, but to accept my legacy
and ardently contribute to our potential, instead of giving
blame to those who lacked the privilege to do great things
with equal zeal…*
*I learned not to run to the dead beats of rage and sorrow,
but to accept my own unique pulsing rhythm of
persistence…*
*I learned not to run from responsibility, but to accept it as
a badge representing the capacity to hold my head high at
the chores of liability…*

Here, I forgive you because in your abandonment you taught a great deal of jazz in your absence dear father.

IRRESPONSIBILITY IS OUR FAILURE

THE END

www.ingramcontent.com/pod-product-compliance
Lightning Source LLC
Chambersburg PA
CBHW031941260626
47157CB00016B/1827